ISLAND HERITAGE™
PUBLISHING
A DIVISION OF THE MADDEN CORPORATION

94-411 Kō'aki Street
Waipahu, Hawai'i 96797-2806
Orders: (800) 468-2800
Information: (808) 564-8800
Fax: (808) 564-8877
islandheritage.com

ISBN: 1-61710-171-0
First Edition, Second Printing—2013
COP 130703

©2012 Island Heritage Publishing. All rights reserved.
No portion of this book may be reproduced in whole or in part
in any form or by any means without prior written permission
from Island Heritage Publishing. Printed in Hong Kong.

Kolohe ʻIole

Written by **Courtnie Chang** • Illustrated by **Ron Borresen**

ISLAND HERITAGE™
PUBLISHING

Kolohe 'Iole was a real rascal rat,

climbing up railings and scaring the cat.

He nibbled on fabric and scratched up a chair.

He sampled the *poke* when no one was there.

❖ Kolohe (koh LOH hay) – mischievous, naughty
❖ 'Iole (ee OH lay) – Hawaiian rat
❖ poke (POH kay) – raw seasoned fish cut into pieces

And when he heard footsteps from outside the door,
he ran to his *hale* up on the third floor.
He lived in an *ipu* that lay on a shelf.
He rested and played there all by himself.

❖ hale (HAH lay) – house; lodge
❖ ipu (EE poo) – bottle gourd used traditionally for storing food or water or as an instrument in dances

His *makuahine* lived right down the hall,
and when she got angry, "Kolohe!" she'd call.
But he never listened, that hard-headed kid.
He kept right on doing the bad things he did.

One day while creeping and sniffing outside,
he saw a large box with two *keiki* inside.
He chuckled a little, then kept on his way
to see if the groceries had come in that day.

But one *keiki* saw him and let out a scream.
"*Auwe*," she cried, "there's a rat on that beam!"
So Kolohe went *holo* up under the eave
and hid 'til he saw the two *keiki* leave.

✤ keiki (KAY kee) – child; children
✤ auwe (OW way) – "oh!"; "oh dear!"
✤ holo (HOH loh) – to run

6

He went to the kitchen and ate up some *poi*,
then went to his *ipu* for some *moemoe*.
Kolohe awoke to a back and forth motion,
a rising and falling like waves in the ocean.

"Now, come in here, *keiki*," he heard a voice say,
"You're not going to see more *'iole* today."
He heard a tap-tapping outside of his gourd
and saw from the *puka* the *keiki* looked bored.

❖ poi (poy) – Hawaiian staple made from crushed taro root
❖ moemoe (moy moy) – rest; sleep
❖ puka (POO kah) – hole; opening

8

"Now," thought Kolohe, "I think I'll have fun.
I'll poke my head out and make those kids run."
That's just what he did, that rascally rat.
The kids and the lady ran this way and that.

He chased down the aunty;
he jumped at a kid.
He frolicked and galloped
and laughed as he did.
Now what that Kolohe had done
was just mean.
Those *keiki* were more scared
than he'd ever seen.

He snickered and chuckled,
then ran out of sight.
He went to bed giggling
and smiling that night.
He thought he was clever,
he thought he was smart.
He knew he would get away
right from the start.

14

And so the next morning Kolohe went out.
He thought it was nothing, him being about.
He thought the two *keiki* were hiding in bed,
but they were out searching for *'iole* instead.

And "*NĀNĀ*!" one called out while still far away,
"I see it, I see it. It's coming this way!"
The *keiki* came charging and Kolohe ran
to the back of the shelf that was next to the fan.

❖ nānā (NAH NAH) - to look at or observe

But when he got there, now what was this mess?
A sticky trap laid by the aunty no less!
He wiggled and waggled 'til his muscles were sore,
but all of the struggling just made him stick more.

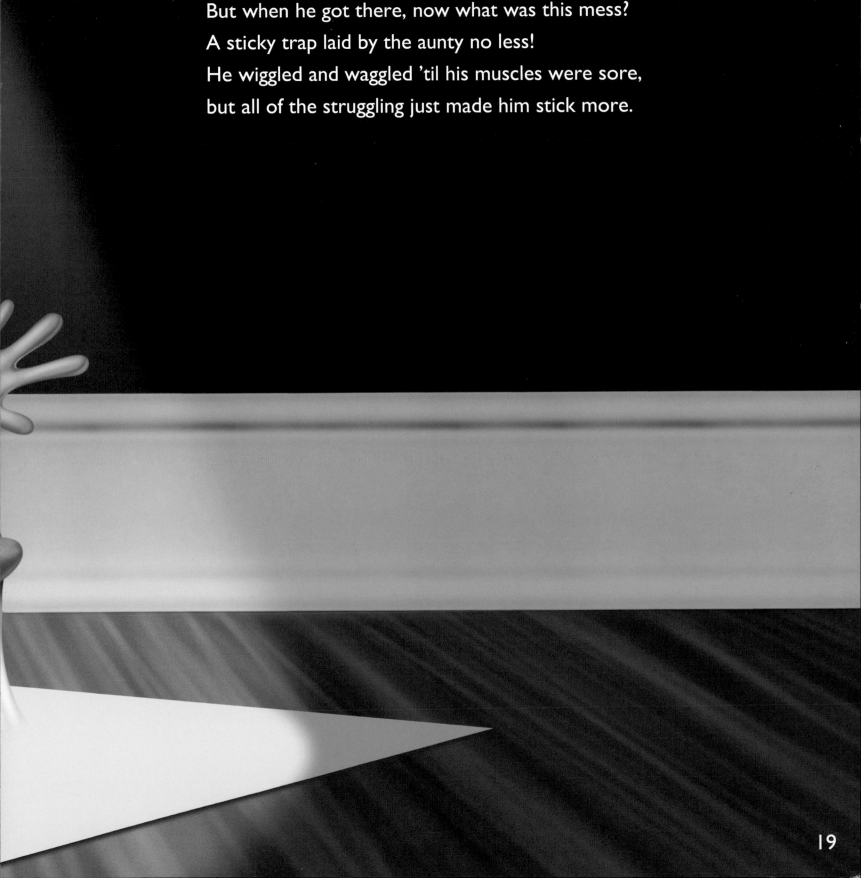

His breathing was heavy,
his eye held a tear.
If he had been good,
there'd be nothing to fear.
But he had been naughty
and now he was scared.
The *keiki* were coming
and they were prepared.

The girl held a jar up, the boy had a stick.
He had to escape from this mess – and quick!
But pulling and pushing had done him no good.
The *keiki* came closer to where the rat stood.

21

just as he started to give up all hope,
his *makuahine* appeared with a rope.
It was really a string, but Kolohe was glad.
His mama had saved him although he'd been bad.

Now Kolohe ʻIole's a good little rat.

He goes upstairs nicely. He's friends with the cat.

No nibbling on fabric or scratching a chair.

Kolohe, *maikaʻi*, you've learned how to care.

❖ maikaʻi (my KAH ee) – good, fine

27

The End